WRITING WITH ZIM

Grades 2-3

SYSTEM DESIGNER

Philip J. Solimene

EDITOR

Deborah Tiersch-Allen

EDCON

Copyright © 1997
Published by

EDCON

30 Montauk Blvd.
Oakdale, New York 11769
(888) 553-3266
Info@edconpublishing.com
www.edconpublishing.com

Printed in U.S.A.
ISBN #1-55576-106-2

Name _____

Thinking About Writing

Zim likes writing. Do you?

Answer each question below.
Take time to think about what you
are writing.

1. What was the last thing you wrote?

_____

2. Did you enjoy writing it? Why or why not?

_____

_____

_____

3. Why do you think it is important for you to be a good writer?

_____

_____

_____

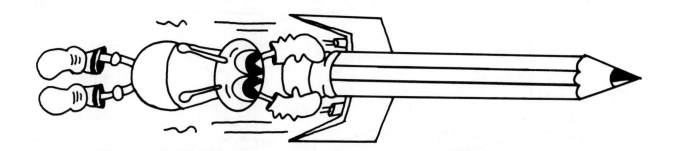

Name _____

More Thinking About Writing

Complete each statement below.

1. The best thing I ever wrote was

_____

2. I think it was good because _____

_____

_____

3. What I like best about writing is _____

_____

_____

Circle each thing that you like to write.

The Writing Process

There are five steps we follow when we write.
These steps are called the Writing Process.

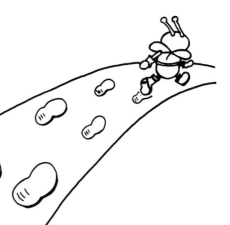

1. Get Ready

Before you start writing, you need to make a plan. You might draw a
picture. You might make a list, a web, a chart, or a story map.
But there is one thing you should always do:

THINK.

Zal is going to write a note to her friend.
Zim is going to write a story about
an exciting space adventure.

Does Zal need to think about what she
will write? _____

Who needs to spend more time thinking and planning? Why?

_____

_____

_____

Name _____

When you start writing, you want to get your IDEAS down on paper.

What you write now is called your **first draft**. You can try things out and change them as much as you want.

@EDCON

THINK about what you want to say and how you want to say it.

What was the most fun you ever had writing? Tell about it.

_____

_____

_____

_____

Skills: critical thinking, making judgments

Name _____

3. Ask for Comments

Zim and Zal talk about Zim's story.
She tells him what she likes about it.
She gives him some ideas for making
it better.

@ EDCON

Why is it a good idea to find out what someone else thinks?
How can talking about your writing help you make it better?

_____

_____

_____

_____

_____

_____

_____

_____

Skills: critical thinking, making judgments

5

Name _____

4. Make Changes

First, Zim changes his story to make it better.

Exciting

Interesting

Then he makes corrections.
- He makes sure his sentences make sense.
- He checks his spelling.
- He makes sure he used capital letters where they belong.
- He checks to see if his sentences end with the right marks.

"I want readers to enjoy and understand what I write."

Think about what Zim wants. Will making changes and corrections help him do that? Why do you think so?

_____

_____

_____

_____

5. Share Your Story

Zim made his story into a book. He drew pictures to go with the words. He made a cover, too.   How do you think he made his book?

_____

_____

_____

Zim wrote a story. He shared it by making it into a book. He might have read it out loud. He might have acted it out with puppets. Think of ways you can share letters, poems or other things that you write. Write down some ideas here.

_____

_____

_____

_____

_____

_____

_____

Skills: critical thinking, generating ideas

Name _____

Writing a Poem — Step 1

1. Get Ready

What would you like to write a poem about? An animal? Your favorite kind of weather? A star? A place you like to go?

Draw a picture here to show what your poem will be about.

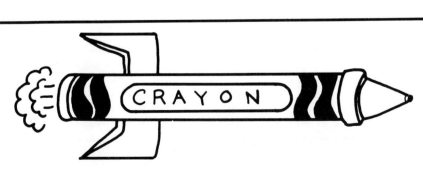

Skills: prewriting (poem)

Name _____

Writing a Poem — Step 1

Write the first draft of your poem on the lines below.
Look at your drawing for ideas.
Remember that a poem does not have to rhyme.

 about what you want to say and how you want to say it.

Name _____

Writing a Poem — Steps 3 and 4

Ask a friend to read your first draft.
Or read your poem out loud to a friend.
Ask what your friend likes about the poem.
Ask for ideas about making it better.

Make notes to help you remember what
you and your friend talk about.

Notes and Comments

_____

_____

_____

_____

_____

_____

- Now look at your poem again. Make the changes you want to make.

- Is your poem just the way you want it?

- Check your spelling.
- Check capital letters and end marks.

- Will readers enjoy and understand your poem?

Skills: conferring, revising, proofreading (poem)

10

Writing a Poem — Step 5

5. Share Your Poem

How will you share your poem?

Make a final copy on good paper.
Write neatly.

Do you want to draw a picture to go
with it?
Do you want to read your poem out
loud?
Do you want to make a book of poems
with your classmates?
Do you have any other ideas?

Tell how you will share your poem.

© EDCON

_____

_____

_____

_____

_____

Name _____

Writing a Description — Step 1

A description tells about something. When you write a description, you tell how something looks. You tell about the color, size, and shape. You might tell what something is made of, what it does, or how it moves. You might also tell how the thing sounds, smells, tastes, or feels.

Choose something you want to describe.

Make a Web

In the box at the center of the web, write the name of what you will describe. In the circles, write words or groups of words you can use to describe it.

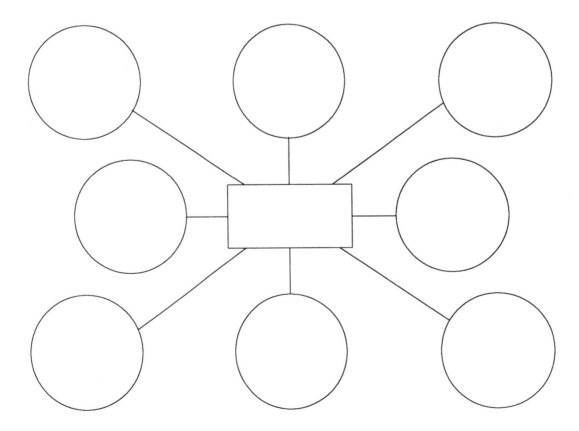

© EDCON

Writing a Description — Step 2

Now write the first draft of your description.

Use words from your web.

If you need more room, use another sheet of paper.

_____

_____

_____

_____

_____

_____

_____

_____

_____

_____

Skills: drafting (description)

Name _____

Writing a Description — Steps 3 and 4

Ask a friend to read your description.
Or read your description out loud to a friend.
Ask what your friend likes about the description.
Ask for ideas about making it better.

Make notes to help you remember what you
and your friend talk about.

Notes and Comments

_____

_____

_____

_____

_____

_____

_____

• Now look at your description again.
  Make the changes you want to make.

• Is your description just the way you want it?

• Check your spelling.
• Check capital letters and end marks.

• Will readers enjoy and understand your
  description?

Writing a Description — Step 5

5. Share Your Description

How will you share your description?

Zim is sharing his as a riddle. He wrote his description on good paper. He left out the name of the thing he described. His friends can read the description and guess what the thing is.

What other ways could you share your description?
Write down some ideas.

_____

_____

_____

_____

_____

_____

_____

Writing a Letter — Step 1

1. Get Ready

Zim wrote a letter to his grandfather. You can write a letter to a friend. It can be a real person or a character from a story.

Who will you write to? _____

What do you want to tell this person?
Make notes below about things you want to say in your letter.

★ ★ ★ ★ ★ ★ ★ ★ ★ ★ ★ ★ ★ ★ ★
★ _____ ★
★ _____ ★
★ _____ ★
★ _____ ★
★ _____ ★
★ _____ ★
★ ★ ★ ★ ★ ★ ★ ★ ★ ★ ★ ★ ★ ★ ★

Skills: prewriting (friendly letter)

16

Name _____

Writing a Letter — Step 2

Write the first draft of your letter.

© EDCON

_____
date

Dear_____
name

_____

_____

_____

_____

_____

_____

_____

Your friend,

_____
your name

Skills: drafting (friendly letter)

17

Name _____

Writing a Letter — Steps 3 and 4

3. Ask for Comments

Ask a partner to read your letter. Or read your letter out loud to your partner.

Ask for ideas to make your letter better.

Make notes to help you remember what you and your partner talk about.

Notes and Comments

_____

_____

_____

_____

_____

4. Make Changes

• Now look at your letter again. Make the changes you want to make.

• Is your letter just the way you want it?

• Check your spelling.
• Check capital letters and end marks.

• Will the person you wrote to enjoy and understand your letter?

Skills: conferring, revising, proofreading (friendly letter)

18

Name _____

Writing a Letter — Step 5

Now you want someone to read your letter. First, make a neat copy with all your changes. You can use special paper or draw pictures.

If you wrote to a friend, maybe you can send your letter. You will need an envelope and a stamp.

Maybe you wrote to a story character. Or maybe you don't know the person's address. You can share your letter with your class-mates or with others. Think of some other ways you might share your letter.

Class Mailbox

_____

_____

_____

_____

_____

_____

Name _____

Writing a Book Report — Step 1

1. Get Ready

A book report is a way to share a book you have read. Choose a story to report on. What will you tell readers about this book? You can use this chart to help you get started.

Title	
Author	
Characters	
What happens in the story.	
What I think about this book.	

Writing a Book Report — Step 2

2. Write Your Book Report

Write the first draft of your book report here.
Use your chart to help you.
If you need more room, use another sheet of paper.

_____

_____

_____

_____

_____

_____

_____

_____

Skills: publishing (friendly letter)

@ EDCON

Name _____

Writing a Book Report
Steps 3 and 4

Ask a friend to read your book report. Or read your book report out loud to your friend. Ask what your friend likes about the book report.

Ask for ideas about making it better.

Make notes to help you remember what you and your friend talk about.

Notes and Comments

_____

_____

_____

_____

_____

- Now look at your book report again. Make the changes you want to make.

- Is your book report just the way you want it?

- Check your spelling.
- Check capital letters and end marks.

- Will readers enjoy and understand your book report?

Skills: conferring, revising, proofreading (book report)

Name _____

Writing a Book Report
Step 5

5. Share Your Book Report

How will you share
your book report?

In Zim's class, book reports go into a special folder.

The folder is in the library corner. Zim and his classmates can check the folder
to find out about books they might want to read.

What are some other ways you can share a book report?

_____

_____

_____

_____

_____

Skills: publishing (book report)

Name _____

Writing a Story — Step 1

1. Get Ready

You can write a story.

Before you start about these things.

1. Who will read your story?

_____

There are many kinds of stories.

Animal Stories   Adventure Stories   Silly Stories   Space Stories

2. What kind of story will you write?

_____

3. How do you want to make your readers feel?

_____

_____

_____

Skills: prewriting (story)

24

Name _____

Writing a Story — More of Step 1

1. Get Ready

What will your story be about?

Will the characters be people? Will they be animals?

What will happen in your story?

How will it begin? What will happen then? How will your story end?

Use the story map below to write down your ideas.

Beginning

Middle

End

© EDCON

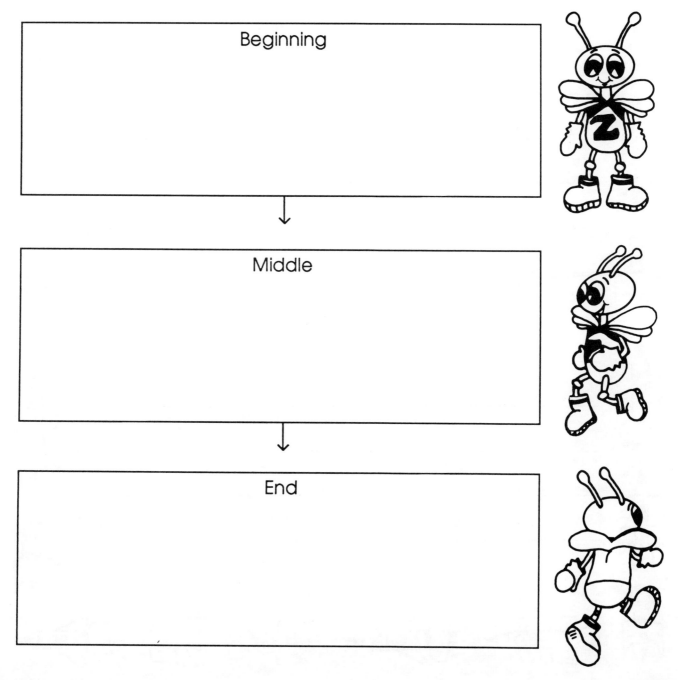

Writing a Story — Step 2

Write the first draft of your story.
Use your story map to help you.
You can go on writing on the next page.

2. Write Your Story

_____

_____

_____

_____

_____

_____

_____

_____

_____

_____

© EDCON

Name _____

Writing a Story — More of Step 2

_____

_____

_____

_____

_____

_____

_____

_____

_____

_____

_____

If you need more room, use another sheet of paper.

Skills: drafting (story)

27

Name _____

Writing a Story — Step 3

Ask a partner to read your story.

Or read your story out loud to a partner.

Ask what your partner likes about the story. Ask for ideas about making it better.

Make notes to help you remember what you and your partner talk about.

Notes and Comments

_____

_____

_____

_____

_____

_____

_____

_____

_____

Skills: conferring (story)

28

© EDCON

Name _____

Writing a Story — Step 4

1. Did talking to your partner give you some good ideas? Are there any changes you want to make in your story? Go back to your first draft and make any changes you want.

2. Pick out an important change you made.
   On the lines below, tell about the change.
   Why and how did you make it?
   How did it make your story better?

_____

_____

_____

_____

_____

_____

_____

_____

_____

3. Is your story just the way you want it?
   Check your spelling, capital letters, and end marks.
   Make corrections to help readers understand what you wrote.

Name _____

Writing a Story — Step 5

There are many ways to share a story.

How will you share your story?
On the lines below, write your plans for sharing your story.
List what you will do and what things you will need.

_____

_____

_____

_____

_____

_____

_____

Skills: publishing (story)

30